Some Things Yo
Know About Goblins

Gaggles
Seven Goblins make a Gaggle.
Not six. Not eight. Seven.

Hats
Goblins always wear woolly
hats with bobbles. They are
very proud of them.

Favourite Food
Sausages.

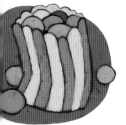

Favourite Sweets
Gobblegum.
And gobstoppers.

Goblin Babies
They eat *anything*.

Kaye Umansky

GOBLINZ!
and THE WITCH

illustrated by Andi Good

PUFFIN

PUFFIN BOOKS

Published by the Penguin Group
Penguin Books Ltd, 80 Strand, London WC2R 0RL, England
Penguin Group (USA) Inc., 375 Hudson Street, New York, New York 10014, USA
Penguin Books Australia Ltd, 250 Camberwell Road, Camberwell, Victoria 3124, Australia
Penguin Books Canada Ltd, 10 Alcorn Avenue, Toronto, Ontario, Canada M4V 3B2
Penguin Books India (P) Ltd, 11 Community Centre, Panchsheel Park, New Delhi – 110 017, India
Penguin Group (NZ), cnr Airborne and Rosedale Roads, Albany, Auckland 1310, New Zealand
Penguin Books (South Africa) (Pty) Ltd, 24 Sturdee Avenue, Rosebank 2196, South Africa

Penguin Books Ltd, Registered Offices: 80 Strand, London WC2R 0RL, England

www.penguin.com

First published 2005
1 3 5 7 9 10 8 6 4 2

Set in Monotype Times New Roman Schoolbook 22 on 14.5pt
Made and printed in China by Midas Printing Ltd

British Library Cataloguing in Publication Data

A CIP catalogue record for this book is available from the British Library

ISBN 0–141–31502–4

Contents

1. Wheels

$\mathbf{I}$t was a hot, blue day and the
Gaggle were down by the muddy
pond.

Oggy and Wheels were wading
about with a bucket, looking for

frogs. Cloreen was hanging upside down from a tree, blowing bubbles. Twinge was making mud pies for his little brother, Grizzle, to eat.

Tuf and Shy just lay side by side on the grass, looking up at the sky.

"What are you thinking about, Tuf?" Shy asked dreamily.

"I is countin' de clouds," said Tuf.
"But there aren't any," said Shy.
"I know. Dat makes it easy."
Just then, there came a loud splash.
"Oops!" Upside-down Cloreen gave
a giggle. "Wheels has fallen in."

Everyone sat up and watched Wheels splashing around. He was holding something big, with wheels. It was covered with pondweed and very rusty.

"What you got there?" called Twinge.

"Wheels," said Wheels proudly, wading ashore. "Just tripped over 'em. *Vrrrrmmmm!*"

"Wow!" said Cloreen. "Let's have a look!"

"It's the bottom bit of an old pram," said Shy. Gingerly, he poked one of the wheels, which squeaked round slowly, dripping mud.

"We could do somethin' with that, couldn't we?" asked Twinge.

"Like what?" said Tuf.

"Like – I dunno. Make something
with wheels on?"

"Like what?"

Twinge shrugged. He couldn't think
of anything. Everyone looked at Shy.
He always came up with ideas.

"What do you t'ink, Shy?" asked Tuf.

"I think," said Shy, running his eyes over the rusty wheels, "*I* think . . ."

"Yeeees?" said the others.

"*I* think we should make a GobbleKart."

"Great! Hooray! A GobbleKart!"
cheered everyone. A little silence fell.
Everyone looked at Tuf, who could
be relied on to ask the right question.

"What dat?" asked Tuf, reliably.

"I saw a picture in a book,"
explained Shy excitedly. "You get in
it and whizz down hills. It'll be fun,

I promise."

"Wow!" everyone gasped.

"What does a GobbleKart look like?" asked Oggy.

"I'll draw it," said Shy. He took a little pad from his pocket. It came with a freshly sharpened pencil with an eraser on. Everyone was very impressed.

They crowded round and looked
over Shy's shoulder as he drew.
What he drew was this:

"Cor!" breathed Tuf. "Dat is *bootiful*."

"So we'll make one," nodded Shy. "It's easy."

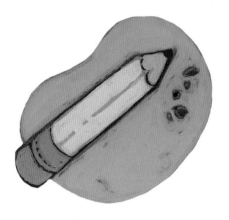

2. The Goat

The goat belonged to Old Ma Musty. It was tied by a fraying piece of string to a washing pole outside her tumbledown hovel. Its name was Bob.

Ma Musty had gone out shopping, forgetting to take in her washing. So far, Bob had eaten two vests, a nighty, three socks, a pillowcase and a pair of drawers off the washing line. All there was left was one lone sock, which he couldn't quite reach.

Bob blew a sigh down his nose and idly chewed his string. He chewed on it quite a lot when he was bored, so it wasn't surprising that it broke.

Hey! Freedom! thought Bob.

Feeling quite frisky, pausing only to snatch the last sock from the line, Bob trotted across the yard, squeezed through the gap in the fence and briskly set off down the hill . . .

The Gaggle stood around surveying their handiwork. Oggy had hurt his finger with the hammer. Cloreen was covered in red paint. Everyone else was hot and sweaty.

Making a GobbleKart was hard work. Borrowing useful tools and finding all the rest of the stuff they needed had taken ages. Putting it all together hadn't been easy either.

"It's not like your drawing, is it?" said Oggy to Shy doubtfully.

"No," agreed Shy. "Not exactly."

Everyone stared at the GobbleKart. Nails stuck out in strange places. It was a bit lopsided.

"The number plate's good, though," said Cloreen.

It was. It said GOB 1 in big red letters.

"What do we do now?" asked
Twinge.

"We'll try it out," said Shy firmly.
"We'll take it up to the top of
Gaspup Hill."

The others gasped.

Gaspup Hill was very steep indeed. Besides, a witch lived up there. Her name was Old Ma Musty. She wasn't fond of Goblins.

"What about Old Ma Musty?" asked Wheels nervously.

"It's daytime. She'll be asleep," said Shy. "We want to try it out, don't we?"

"How do we get it there?" asked Twinge.

"It's got wheels," Shy pointed out. "We'll take turns steering it while the others push."

"What about Grizzle?" asked Twinge. "He's too little to steer or push, aren't you, Gr– hey! Where's Grizzle?"

*

Grizzle was toddling along the lane,
singing to himself. He was bored with
making a GobbleKart. Nobody would
let him use the saw. He was bored with
eating mud too. He had had an all-mud
breakfast and now he was ready for
something different for lunch. Something
that wasn't brown.

"Ga," sang Grizzle merrily. "Gaga
gaga ga!"

He spotted a clump of buttercups.
Mmm. Yellow. He grabbed a
handful, sat down in the road and
began stuffing them into his mouth.

Just then, who should come trotting
round the corner but – Bob!

Bob stopped in his tracks.

Grizzle looked up, mouth full of
soggy flowers.

They stared at each other.

Then Grizzle held out a handful of buttercups, gave a bright smile and said: "Ga?"

Bob didn't need asking twice.

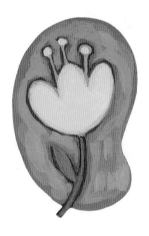

3. Pushing the GobbleKart

"**G**rizzle!" Shy was shouting. "Where are you, Gr– oh, there you are!"

Bob and Grizzle turned to look at

him. They had eaten all the
buttercups and moved on to clover.

Shy put his fingers in his mouth
and gave a loud whistle.

"Found him!" he shouted. "He's
here, in the lane. With a goat!"

A moment later, everyone else
came trudging up, with the rattling
GobbleKart in tow.

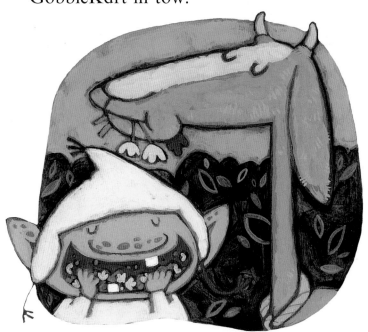

"Bad baby!" scolded Twinge, scooping Grizzle into his arms.

"Ga," said Grizzle, reaching down and patting Bob, who gave him a friendly lick then carried on munching.

"Yes, I know it's a goat. But you're not to go off on your own."

"What a goat doing in de lane anyway?" asked Tuf.

Everyone stared at Bob. Bob stared steadily back, chewing.

"Old Ma Musty's got a goat," said Wheels. "But she keeps it in her yard. *Vrmmmm!*"

"Can't be de same one, den," said Tuf. "Cos dis one's here."

"But supposing it *is* hers?" pondered Shy. "Shouldn't we take it back?"

"Never mind the goat," said Oggy. "Let's get going. Who's riding first?"

"Cloreen," said Shy. "She's the lightest, after Grizzle."

So Cloreen climbed into the GobbleKart and picked up the steering rope. Everyone else got behind it.

"One, two, three – push!" said Shy.

Everyone pushed. The GobbleKart
rolled a short way before one of the
front wheels came up against a stone.

"Steer, Cloreen!" shouted Oggy
crossly. "Pull the rope to the left!"

"I am!" yelled Cloreen, pulling to

the right. "Push harder, can't you?"

Everyone pushed harder. The GobbleKart lurched over the stone, rolled on again, then became bogged down in a clump of grass.

"This is silly," gasped Shy. "We'll

never get to Gaspup Hill at this rate.
It'll take us a week just to push it up
the lane. Unless . . ."

He broke off. His eyes were on
Bob, who was now tucking into a
bramble bush.

"Unless what?" asked Tuf, fanning
himself with his bobble hat.

"I've got an idea . . ." said Shy.

4. Looking for Bob

Old Ma Musty arrived back at her hovel feeling hot, tired and grumpy. Usually, she slept most of the day and only went out when the moon was up. But she had run out of all the basics – tea, sugar, goat pellets, cauldron powder, broom oil

and chocolate biscuits – and there was
nothing for it but to go shopping.

Down in the village, she had to
queue for everything and they only
had custard creams, which she didn't
much like. It had taken her ages to
toil back up the hill with her heavy

bags. She was not in a good mood.

The moment she walked into the
yard, she knew something was wrong.

"Blow me!" cried Old Ma Musty,
stopping short. "Where's me
drawers?"

Vests, nightgown, pillowcase,

drawers – all the washing had vanished from the line! And where was Bob? All that was left of him was a broken piece of string.

"Bob!" shouted Ma Musty. "Where are you, Bobby boy?"

There was no answering bleat.

"Robbed!" hissed Ma Musty. "Thieves have been here and pinched my washing and got my goat! Mess with me, would they? We'll see about that!"

She gave her wand a brisk little shake. A few green sparks fizzed briefly at the tip. Good. It was fully charged. Now for the spell.

"*Magic Wand, now do your job!*

Find my goat. His name is Bob!" chanted Ma Musty.

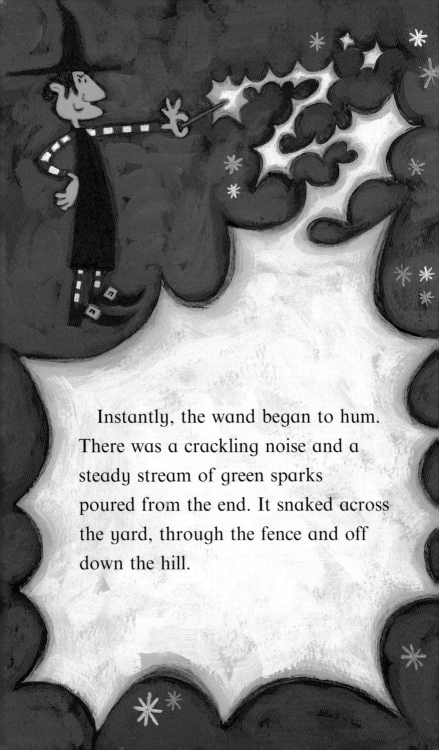

Instantly, the wand began to hum.
There was a crackling noise and a
steady stream of green sparks
poured from the end. It snaked across
the yard, through the fence and off
down the hill.

With a determined glint in her eye, and her wand held stiffly before her, Ma Musty followed . . .

5. Bob Pulls the GobbleKart

Getting Bob to pull the GobbleKart was not easy. It needed a lot of teamwork.

First, they had to get Bob to stand still while they attached the rope to the bit of frayed string trailing from his collar. The only way they could do that was to keep him eating.

Twinge, Wheels and Cloreen raced to and fro with tempting armfuls of greenery. Bob sampled them all. So did Grizzle. That left Oggy, Tuf and Shy to harness Bob to the GobbleKart without him noticing.

When Bob finally did notice, he was a bit peeved. What was the point of escaping if he had to pull things? He stamped a hoof and went into a sulk.

"We'll have to keep the food coming," said Shy. "We'll pick all his favourites and walk in front of him and make encouraging noises. He's so

greedy, he's sure to follow. We'll draw straws to see who goes first in the GobbleKart."

Oggy picked the shortest straw. He climbed in carefully, avoiding the nails. Grizzle rode on Bob's back, while Twinge walked alongside, to make sure Grizzle didn't fall off.

Grizzle clutched hold of Bob's neck,

giggling like mad.

Everyone else walked on ahead, waggling branches and waving handfuls of dandelions around.

It worked. Slowly, neck outstretched towards the tempting snacks, Bob moved up the lane. The GobbleKart rattled and squeaked and jolted along behind, with Oggy clinging on grimly, complaining loudly about the nails.

Down, down the steep track came

the ribbon of green sparks, twirling
as it came, winding round corners,
almost seeming to sniff the air.

   A short distance behind came Old
Ma Musty, following the trail,
muttering things like: "Robbed! At my
age!" and "Mother's coming, Bob,"

and "I'll get 'em, see if I don't," and "If they've touched one hair of his beard . . ."

6. The Witch

"Well, here we are, then," puffed Cloreen. "Gaspup Hill. Are we ready?"

Everyone stopped and wiped their brows. The lane had been bad enough. But the hill was something else altogether. Up, up rose the rough track, like a giant slide.

Bob looked at the hill. Old Ma Musty would be back by now. She would have discovered the missing washing. No. He didn't want to go up there.

He stamped a hoof, shook his head and went into reverse. Grizzle gave a thrilled little squeal and clutched at his horns.

Wheels hastily held out a juicy
dock leaf, which acted as a brake.
Bob changed his mind and came to a
halt. He never backed away from
food.

"Whose turn is
it to ride?" asked
Tuf, climbing out
of the GobbleKart.

Everybody had
had a go at being
towed in the Kart,
apart from
Grizzle. It was a
very bumpy ride.
The number plate
kept falling off
and the nails dug
in unless you sat

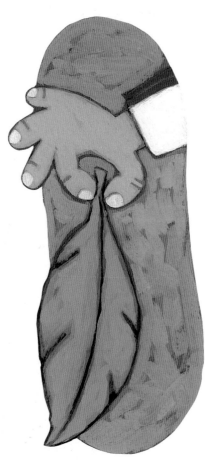

in a certain position. But at least you were sitting. It was better than walking backwards, feeding Bob.

"My turn," said Shy.

He clambered into the GobbleKart and the long haul up Gaspup Hill began.

Down poured the river of green sparks . . . searching . . . seeking . . .

Up toiled the Goblineers, busily keeping Bob stoked up . . .

Until . . . about halfway up . . .

They met!

It happened really quickly. The river of sparks came swooping round the bend and aimed straight for Bob, who looked a bit surprised and choked on a daisy. It circled triumphantly round his head, fizzing and crackling as the Gaggle dived into the bushes for cover. And then –

"Aha!" squawked a furious voice. "Nasty little Goblins! I might have known!"

And round the bend marched Old Ma Musty.

"Ah," said Shy. "It's you, Mrs Musty. Er – is this your goat . . .?"

But Old Ma Musty was furious. She didn't want to talk. She wanted revenge.

She gave her wand a twiddle. The green sparks stopped whooshing round Bob's head, concentrated themselves into a thin, laser-like line – and briskly cut through the rope that attached the GobbleKart to Bob!

"Ahhhh . . ." began Shy, as he found himself rolling backwards. His horrified eyes bulged as he picked up speed. One moment, Old Ma Musty was right in front of him, the next she

was a long, long, long way away.

Down, down, down sped poor Shy,
faster and faster. The wind whizzed
past his ears, threatening to snatch
his hat off.

"Oooooh!" he wailed as the

GobbleKart hurtled round the first bend.

"Eeeeee!" he screamed as it took the second on two wheels.

"Ow-ow-ow-ow!" he stuttered as it hit a stony patch.

"Nooooo!" he squawked as he careered backwards down the last steep bit . . .

along the lane . . .

under the stile . . .

over the bridge . . .

and into the muddy pond!

7. So Was It Fun?

"I likes custard creams," said Tuf, chewing happily. "Even stale ones."

It was the following day. They all sat in the Club House passing around the tin of biscuits. Old Ma Musty had

sent them down to say sorry for
making a mistake about Bob and the
washing.

Besides, she didn't like custard
creams much.

"Ma Musty was glad to get Bob

back, wasn't she?" said Oggy, helping
himself to two.

"And she did say sorry about my
muddy clothes," said Shy, taking three.

"Shame about the GobbleKart,
though," said Wheels.

"Yeah. It was a brilliant idea," said Tuf. "Do you think we can patch it up?"

Silence fell.

"Do we want to?" asked Cloreen.

Everyone thought about this.

"My thumb still hurts from the first

time," said Oggy.

"As for those nails . . ." agreed
Twinge.

"And we won't have Bob next
time . . ."

"Besides," added
Cloreen, with a
shudder. "Besides,
going down
the hill
backwards
looked really
scary."

"It was," said
Shy, with a little
shiver. "It was fast and
scary and horrible."

"But was it fun?" asked Wheels.

"Ye . . . ee . . . sss. Sort of.

But I never want to do it again."

"So what shall we do instead?" asked Oggy.

"Go back to my house for sausages?" suggested Tuf.

Now, that *was* a brilliant idea.